ALIENS LOVE UNDERPANTS AND...

Birthdays, Sports and Holidays

SIMON & SCHUSTER

First published in Great Britain in 2019 by
Simon & Schuster UK Ltd
1st Floor, 222 Gray's Inn Road, London WC1X 8HB
A CBS Company

Text and illustrations copyright © Aliens Love Underpants And... © Tiger Aspect Productions Ltd 2017.

Based on the Aliens Love Underpants book series written by Claire Freedman and illustrated by Ben Cort

Adapted from the Sky Kids series Aliens Love Underpants And... © Sky UK Limited (2017)
Music and lyrics by David Schweitzer. Director Steve Edge. Producer Tom Beattie.

A CIP catalogue record for this book is available from the British Library upon request

PB ISBN: 978-1-4711-8050-7   eBook ISBN: 978-1-4711-8051-4
Printed in China   10 9 8 7 6 5 4 3 2 1

The inclusion of author or illustrator website addresses in this book
does not constitute an endorsement by or an association with
Simon & Schuster UK Ltd of such sites or the content, products,
advertising or other materials presented on such sites.

Scan this QR code to download your 3 songs:

Birthdays, Sports and Holidays

SIMON & SCHUSTER

London   New York   Sydney   Toronto   New Delhi

Aliens Love Underpants and . . .

BIRTHDAYS

Happy birthday,
Aliens in underpants, we all say
Happy birthday,
Shout it out across the Milky Way.

If you wish your birthday was sooner,
Visit us on planet Pantaloon!
Aliens who live round here

Have thirty-three birthdays every year!
Yes, it's like a dream come true,
Tomorrow I'll be one thousand and two.

That's a big cake without a doubt,
But it's hard to blow the candles out!

It's an alien party and we're so excited.
From Jupiter to Mars, everybody's invited.
With party hats, ginormous balloons,
Dancing on the moon to our favourite tunes.

Pass the parcel that never ends!
Jelly and ice cream with all of your friends.

A present for me,
Oh thank you, guys . . .

UNDERPANTS!
Well, what a surprise.

Happy birthday,
Aliens in underpants, we all say
Happy birthday,
Shout it out across the Milky Way.

Happy birthday, (Come on everybody!)
Aliens in underpants, we all say
Happy birthday, (Come on everybody!)
Shout it out across the Milky Way.

Aliens Love Underpants and . . .

SPORTS

Today is your big day
To be the best of the Milky Way.

You've been training for so long,
You just gotta keep strong.

This is the one for sure,
That you've been waiting for.

Win or lose, give it your best shot -
Give everything you've got!

You're gonna run so fast, (Superspeed!)
Gonna jump so high, (Mega-high!)
Keep it up and you can touch the sky!

You'll hear the crowd go wild from outer space,

COME ON!

Can't wait to play the game
Fun is your middle name.
On your own or as a team,
You're gonna live the dream!

The time has come around,
Gravity won't hold you down.
Your star is shining bright,
You're quicker than the speed of light!

So get ready, get steady, get on your feet.
Come on and move your body to an alien beat!
You might even win it, with something to prove,
On your marks, get set, it's time to move.

Give a little sweat, give a little heart.
Gotta get warmed up, get ready to start.

It's gonna be hard, yes it's gonna be tough,
But aliens in underpants don't give up!

Aliens Love Underpants and . . .
HOLIDAYS

We're going on holiday, we're leaving in a minute,
So grab your suitcase and throw everything in it.

We got no school, hip hip hooray!
Must be time for a holiday!

We're packing our underpants, what else do we need?
Snacks and swimming things, something to read.

It's gonna be awesome,
It's gonna be fun.
The planet we're off to
Is right next to the sun!

Strange food on the menu, things aren't what they seem.
Slime-covered pudding with a scoop of ice cream!

Discover new places, discover new things.
You never know what a holiday brings.

A day at the beach just splashing and lazing,
Alien sandcastles are so amazing.
It's gonna be awesome, it's gonna be great.
We can all have a lie-in so let's stay up late!

We're going on holiday, we're leaving in a minute,
So grab your suitcase and throw everything in it.
We got no school, hip hip hooray!
Must be time for a holiday!

HOLIDAYS!

And don't forget your underpants!